ABOUT KUMON

KUMON®
MATH. READING. SUCCESS.

What is Kumon?

Kumon is the world's largest supplemental education provider and a leader in producing outstanding results. After-school programs in math and reading at Kumon Centers around the globe have been helping children succeed for 50 years.

Kumon Workbooks represent just a fraction of our complete curriculum of preschool-to-college-level material assigned at Kumon Centers under the supervision of trained Kumon Instructors.

The Kumon Method enables each child to progress successfully by practicing material until concepts are mastered and advancing in small, manageable increments. Instructors carefully assign materials and pace advancement according to the strengths and needs of each individual student.

Students usually attend a Kumon Center twice a week and practice at home the other five days. Assignments take about twenty minutes.

Kumon helps students of all ages and abilities master the basics, improve concentration and study habits, and build confidence.

How did Kumon begin?

IT ALL BEGAN IN JAPAN 50 YEARS AGO when a parent and teacher named Toru Kumon found a way to help his son Takeshi do better in school. At the prompting of his wife, he created a series of short assignments that his son could complete successfully in less than 20 minutes a day and that would ultimately make high school math easy. Because each was just a bit more challenging than the last, Takeshi was able to master the skills and gain the confidence to keep advancing.

This unique self-learning method was so successful that Toru's son was able to do calculus by the time he was in the sixth grade. Understanding the value of good reading comprehension, Mr. Kumon then developed a reading program employing the same method. His programs are the basis and inspiration of those offered at Kumon Centers today under the expert guidance of professional Kumon Instructors.

Mr. Toru Kumon
Founder of Kumon

What can Kumon do for my child?

Kumon is geared to children of all ages and skill levels. Whether you want to give your child a leg up in his or her schooling, build a strong foundation for future studies or address a possible learning problem, Kumon provides an effective program for developing key learning skills given the strengths and needs of each individual child.

What makes Kumon so different?

Kumon uses neither a classroom model nor a tutoring approach. It's designed to facilitate self-acquisition of the skills and study habits needed to improve academic performance. This empowers children to succeed on their own, giving them a sense of accomplishment that fosters further achievement. Whether for remedial work or enrichment, a child advances according to individual ability and initiative to reach his or her full potential. Kumon is not only effective, but also surprisingly affordable.

What is the role of the Kumon Instructor?

Kumon Instructors regard themselves more as mentors or coaches than teachers in the traditional sense. Their principal role is to provide the direction, support and encouragement that will guide the student to performing at 100% of his or her potential. Along with their rigorous training in the Kumon Method, all Kumon Instructors share a passion for education and an earnest desire to help children succeed.

KUMON FOSTERS:

- A mastery of the basics of reading and math
- Improved concentration and study habits
- Increased self-discipline and self-confidence
- A proficiency in material at every level
- Performance to each student's full potential
- A sense of accomplishment

▶▶ GETTING STARTED IS EASY. Just call us at 877.586.6671 or visit kumon.com to request our free brochure and find a Kumon Center near you. We'll direct you to an Instructor who will be happy to speak with you about how Kumon can address your child's particular needs and arrange a free placement test. There are more than 1,700 Kumon Centers in the U.S. and Canada, and students may enroll at any time throughout the year, even summer. Contact us today.

FIND OUT MORE ABOUT KUMON MATH & READING CENTERS.
Receive a free copy of our parent guide, *Every Child an Achiever,* by visiting
kumon.com/go.survey or calling **877.586.6671**

Review of Alphabet
Writing a-z

To parents
Write your child's name and the date in the boxes above. On pages 1 and 2, your child will review the letters of the alphabet. Please help your child as needed and praise him or her at the completion of each exercise.

■ Trace the letters a to z.

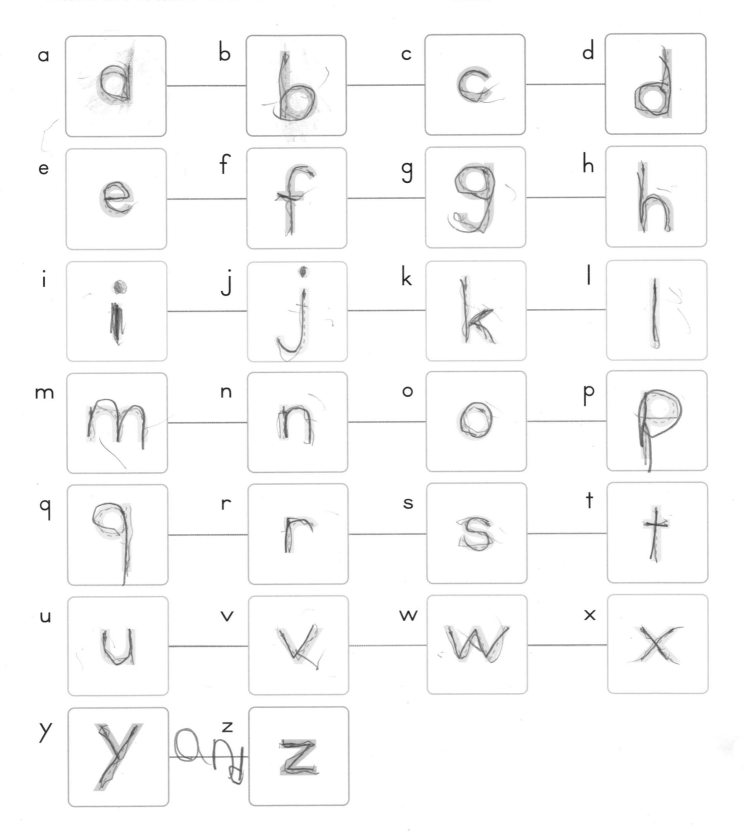

■ Trace the letters a to z.

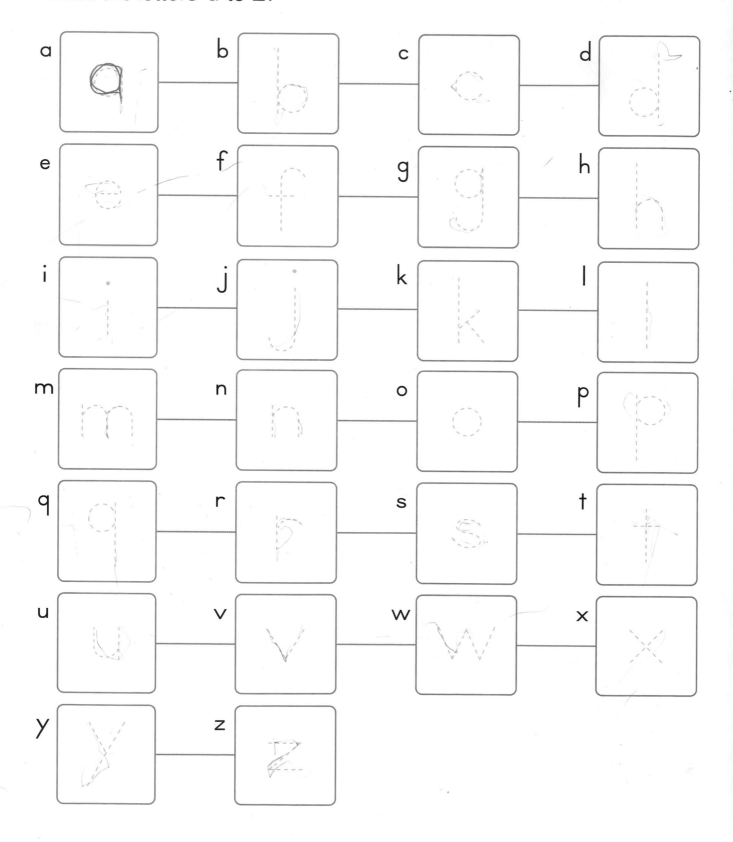

What Is It?

Saying "_at" Sounds

Name
Jackson
Date
Sept. 26, 2007

To parents
By repeating rhyming words with the short "a" vowel sound, your child will gain an awareness of the connection between letters and the sounds they represent. Give your child plenty of encouragement and praise your child at the completion of each exercise.

■ Match the pictures by drawing a line from the dot (●) to the star (★).

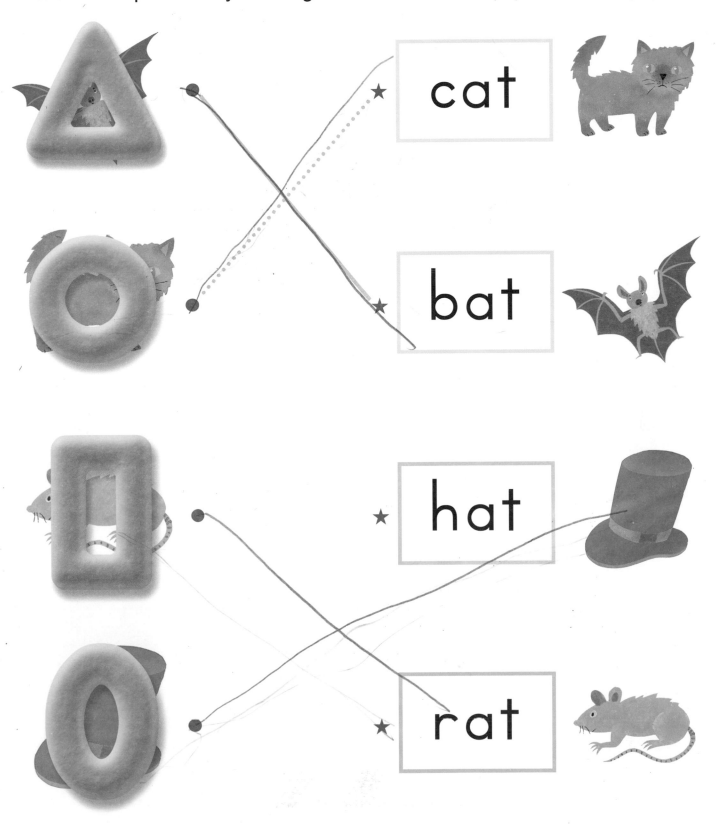

■ Draw a line from the dot (●) to the star (★) while saying each word.

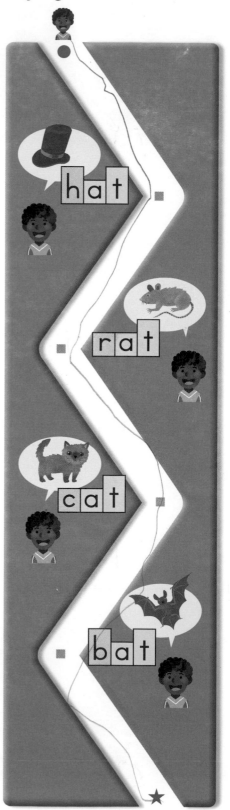

Name
Jackson

Date
Sept. 26, 2007

To parents
Please help your child to say the sound of the individual letters as he or she traces them. Children should not be forced to blend the letters together or to try sounding out the words. If children are allowed to demonstrate their skills naturally, after they have had sufficient practice, then they will have more positive feelings about independent learning.

■ Say the word. Then say the sound of each letter as you trace it.

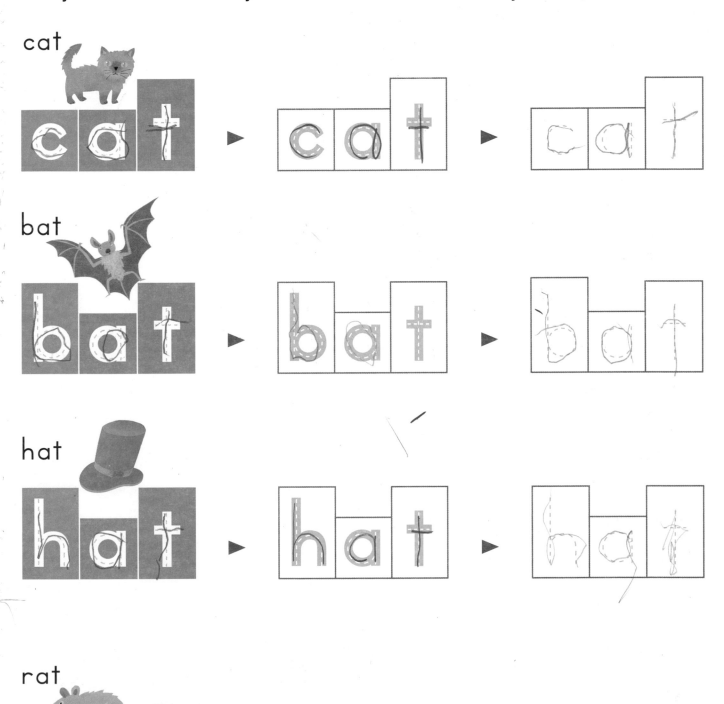

cat

bat

hat

rat

■ Say the word. Then say the sound of each letter as you trace and write it.

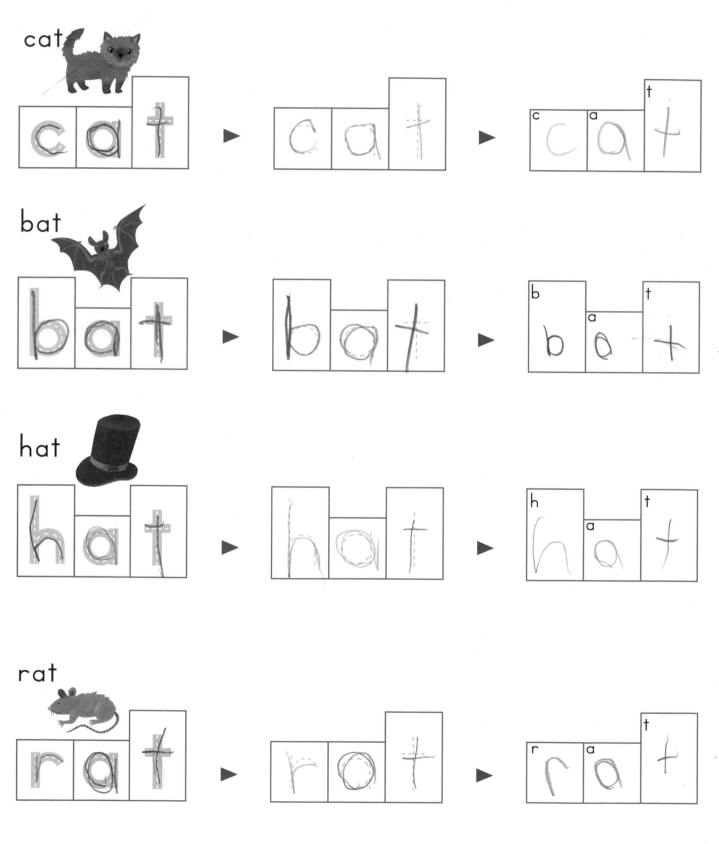

4 What Is It?
Saying "_an" Sounds

Name

Date

■ Match the pictures by drawing a line from the dot (●) to the star (★).

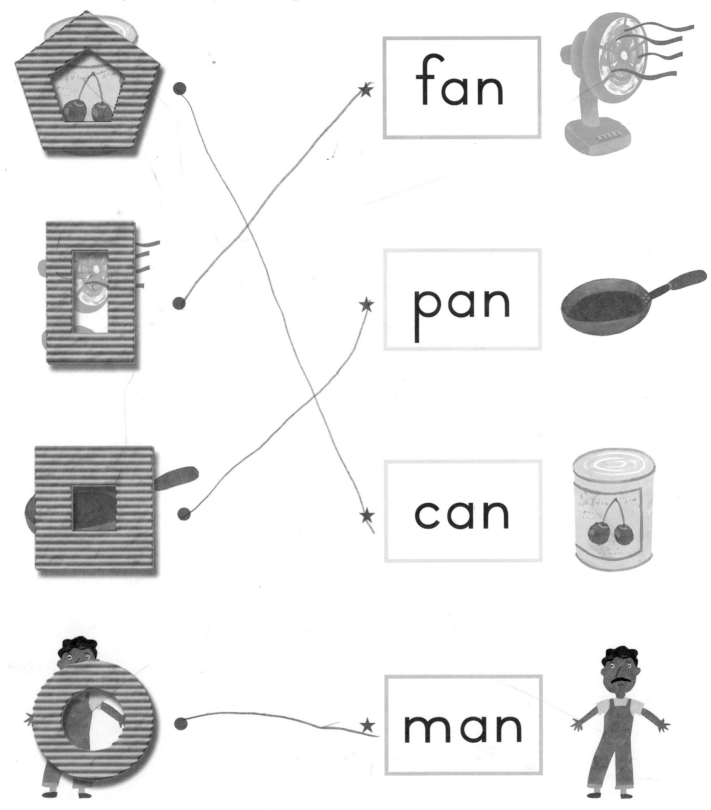

■ Draw a line from the dot (●) to the star (★) while saying each word.

Rhyming Words

Writing "_an" Words

Name Poppy

Date 27

■ Say the word. Then say the sound of each letter as you trace it.

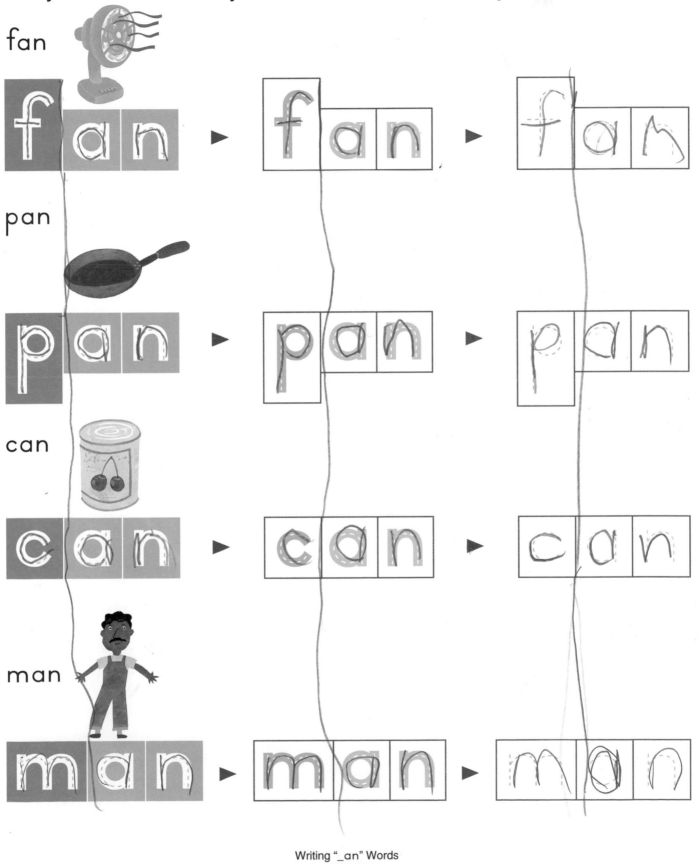

fan

pan

can

man

■ Say the word. Then say the sound of each letter as you trace and write it.

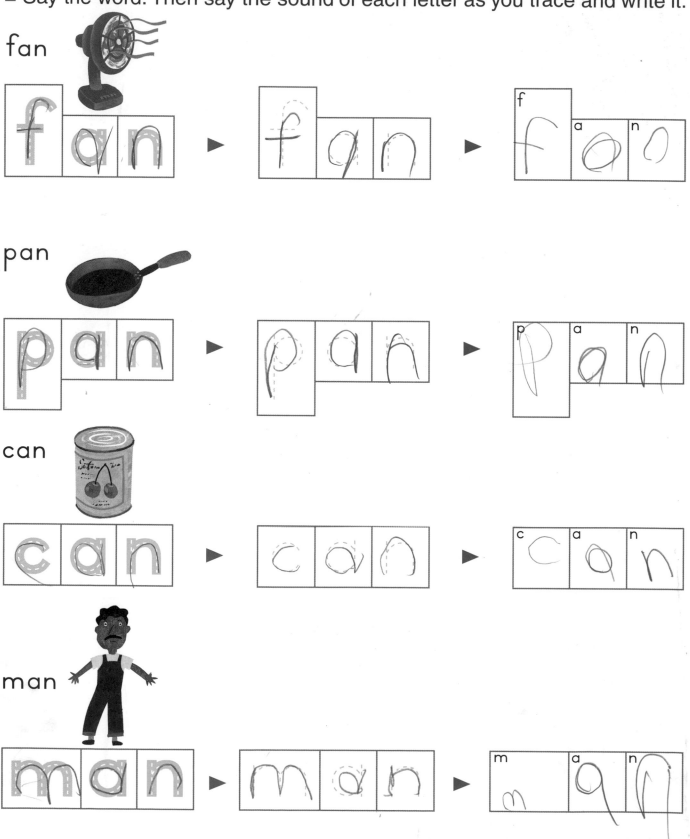

fan

pan

can

man

What Is It?
Saying "_ap" Sounds

■ Match the pictures by drawing a line from the dot (●) to the star (★).

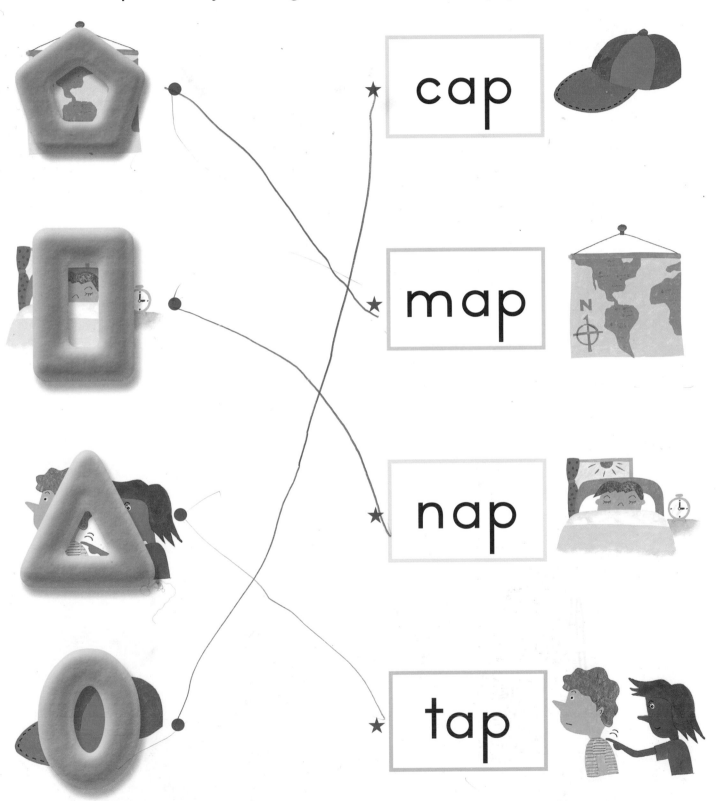

■ Draw a line from the dot (●) to the star (★) while saying each word.

Rhyming Words
Writing "_ap" Words

Name Peppy

Date 3-18-19

■ Say the word. Then say the sound of each letter as you trace it.

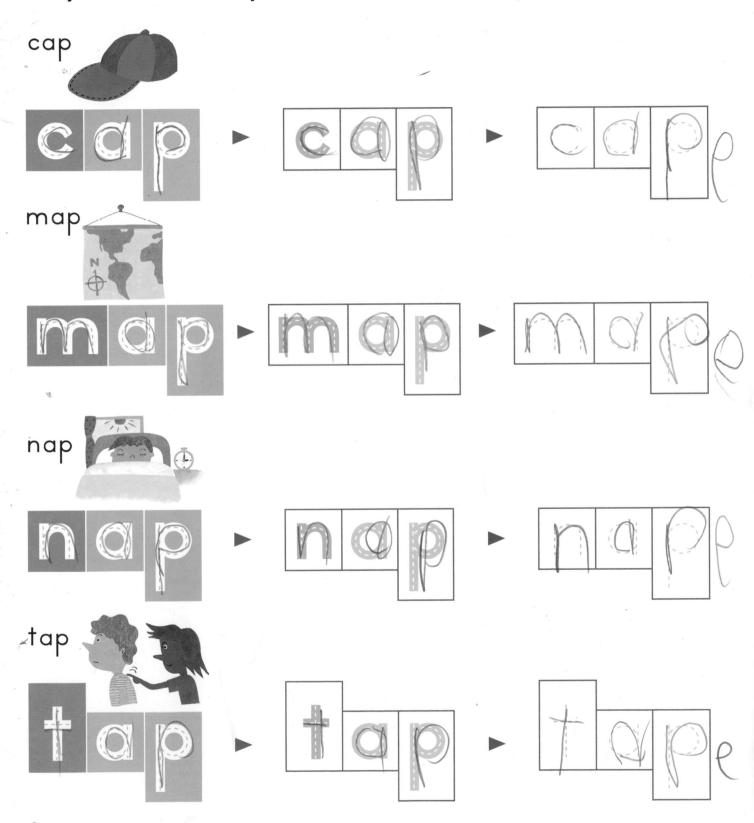

cap

map

nap

tap

■ Say the word. Then say the sound of each letter as you trace and write it.

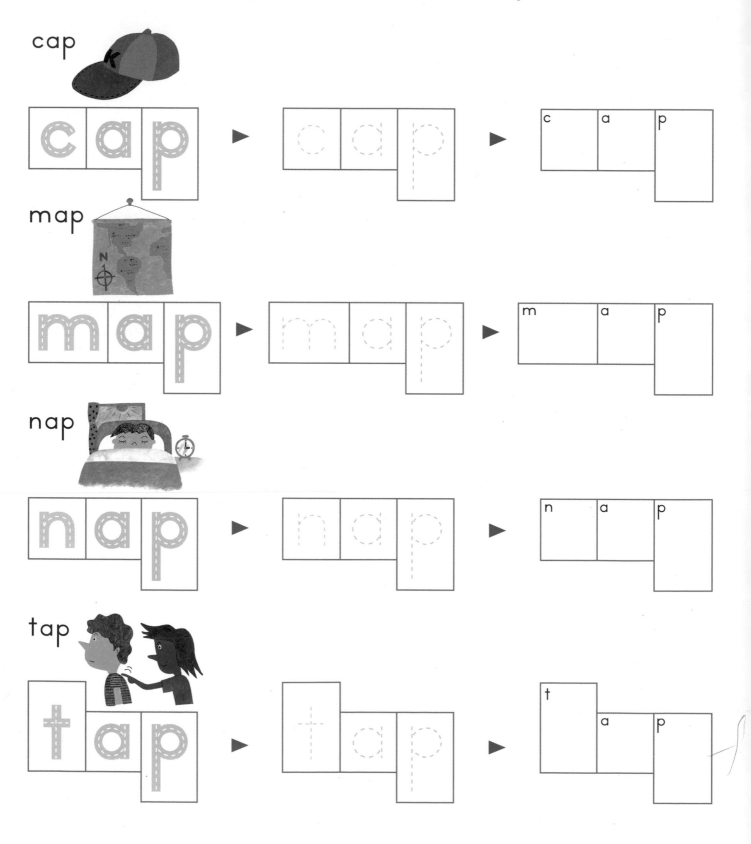

cap

map

nap

tap

What Is It?
Saying "_ad" Sounds

Name

Date

■ Match the pictures by drawing a line from the dot (●) to the star (★).

 ●

★

 ●

★

 ●

★

 ●

★

■ Draw a line from the dot (●) to the star (★) while saying each word.

■ Say the word. Then say the sound of each letter as you trace it.

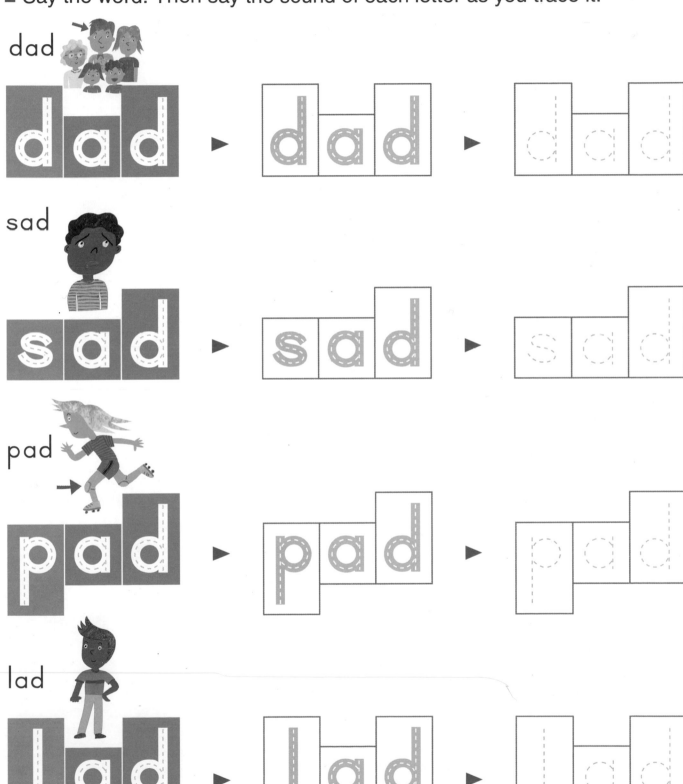

■ Say the word. Then say the sound of each letter as you trace and write it.

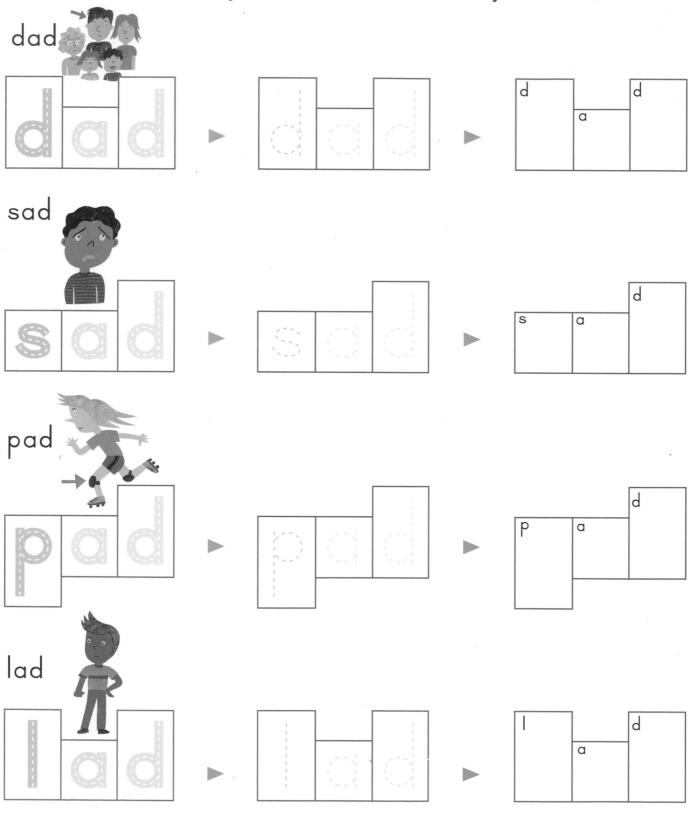

Name

Date

■ Draw a line from  to while saying each "_at" word.
  Draw a line from to while saying each "_an" word.

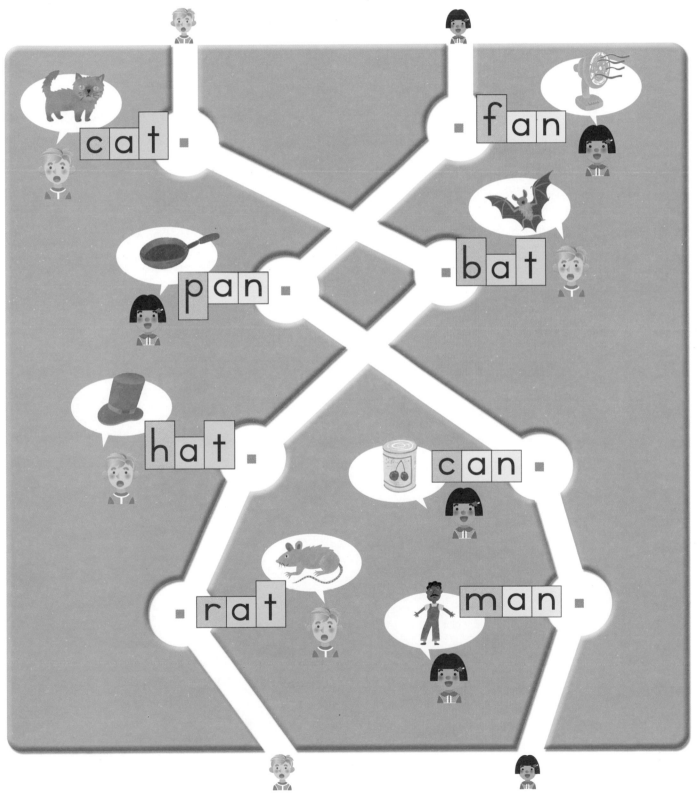

Writing "_at" and "_an" Words

■ Say the word. Then say the sound of each letter as you write it.

cat

| c | a | t |

fan

| f | a | n |

bat

| b | a | t |

pan

| p | a | n |

hat

| h | a | t |

can

| c | a | n |

rat

| r | a | t |

man

| m | a | n |

Review

Saying "_ap" and "_ad" Words

Name

Date

■ Draw a line from 👦 to 👦 while saying each "_ap" word.

Draw a line from 👧 to 👧 while saying each "_ad" word.

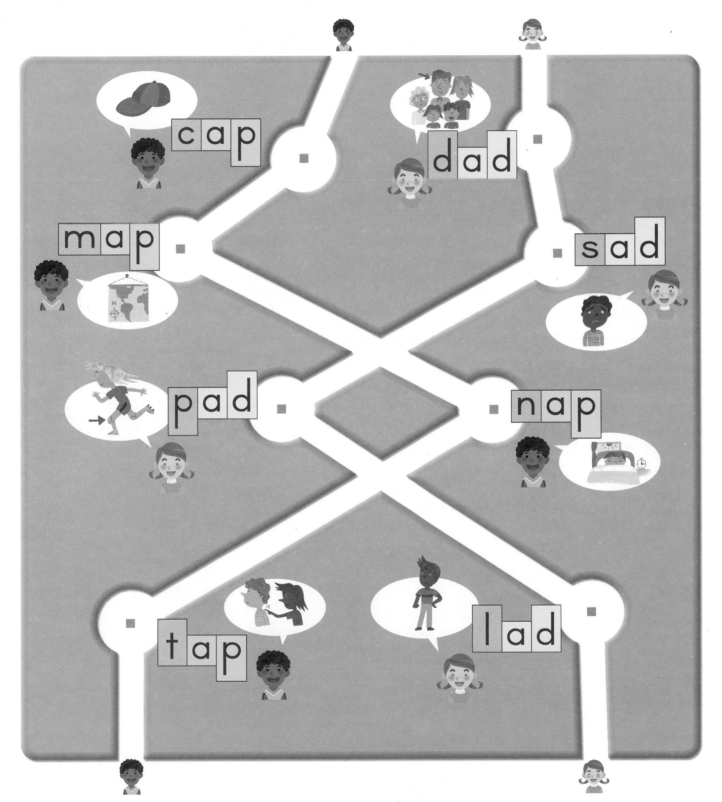

Writing "_ap" and "_ad" Words

■ Say the word. Then say the sound of each letter as you write it.

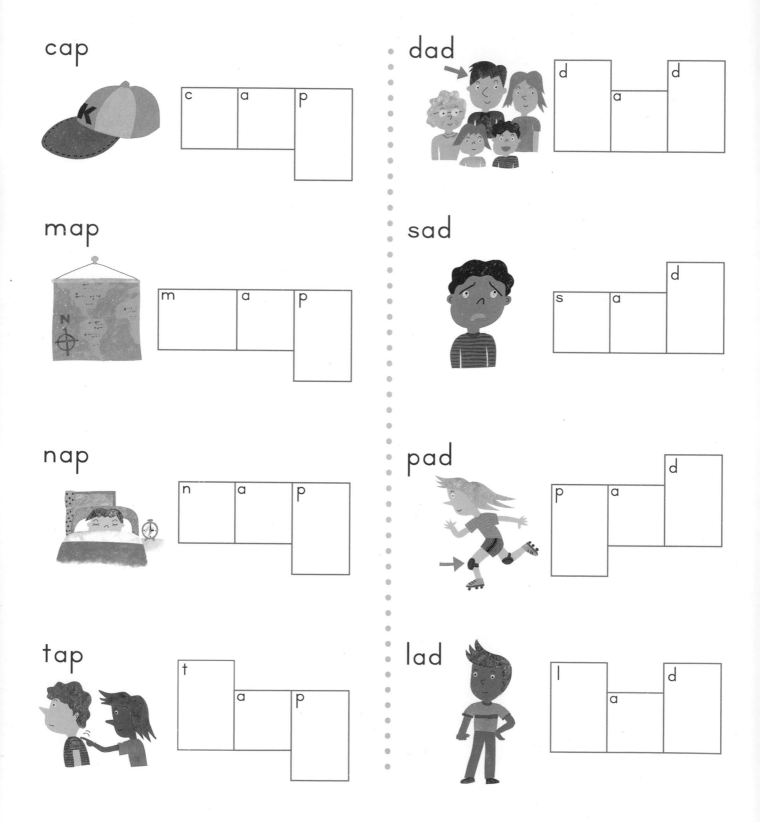

cap

| c | a | p |

map

| m | a | p |

nap

| n | a | p |

tap

| t | a | p |

dad

| d | a | d |

sad

| s | a | d |

pad

| p | a | d |

lad

| l | a | d |

What Is It?

Saying "_en" Sounds

To parents
By repeating rhyming words with the short "e" vowel sound, your child will gain an awareness of the connection between letters and the sounds they represent.

■ Match the pictures by drawing a line from the dot (●) to the star (★).

★  pen

★ men

★ hen

★ ten

■ Draw a line from the dot (●) to the star (★) while saying each word.

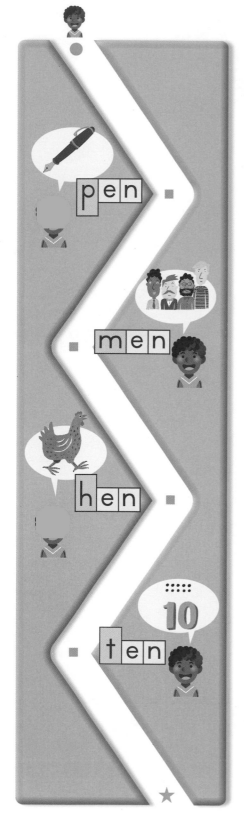

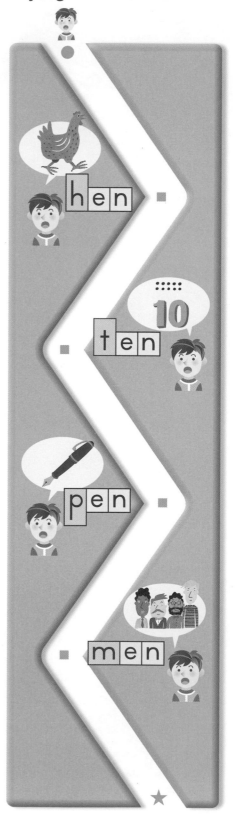

13 Rhyming Words
Writing "_en" Words

Name

Date

■ Say the word. Then say the sound of each letter as you trace it.

pen

men

hen

ten

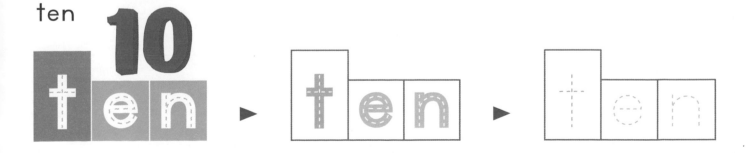

■ Say the word. Then say the sound of each letter as you trace and write it.

pen

men

hen

ten

What Is It?
Saying "_et" Sounds

■ Match the pictures by drawing a line from the dot (●) to the star (★).

 ●

★  **net**

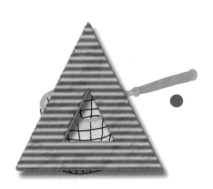 ●

★ **wet**

 ●

★ **pet**

 ●

★ **get**

■ Draw a line from the dot (●) to the star (★) while saying each word.

Saying "_et" Sounds

Rhyming Words
Writing "_et" Words

■ Say the word. Then say the sound of each letter as you trace it.

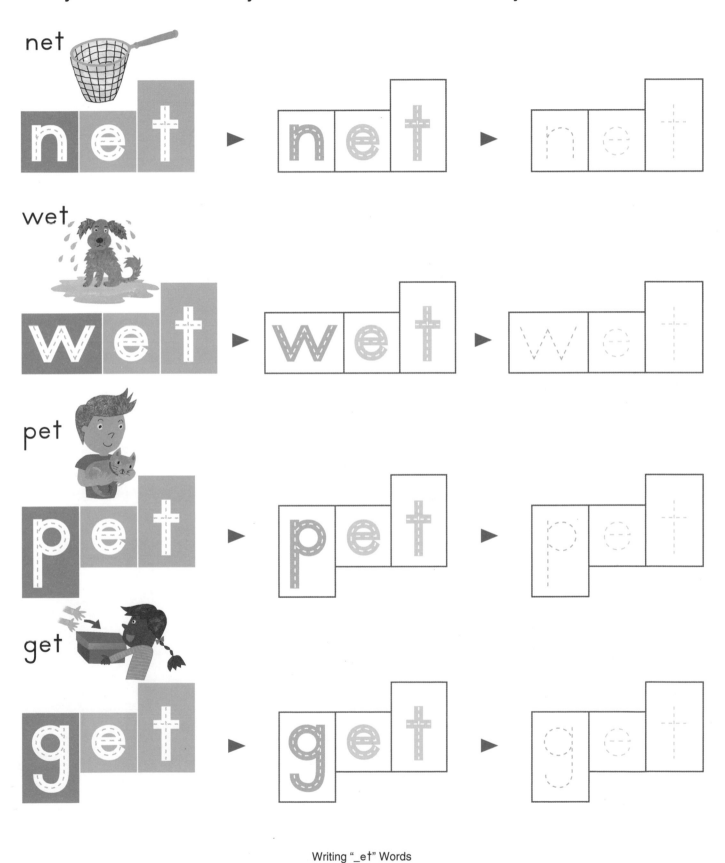

net

wet

pet

get

■ Say the word. Then say the sound of each letter as you trace and write it.

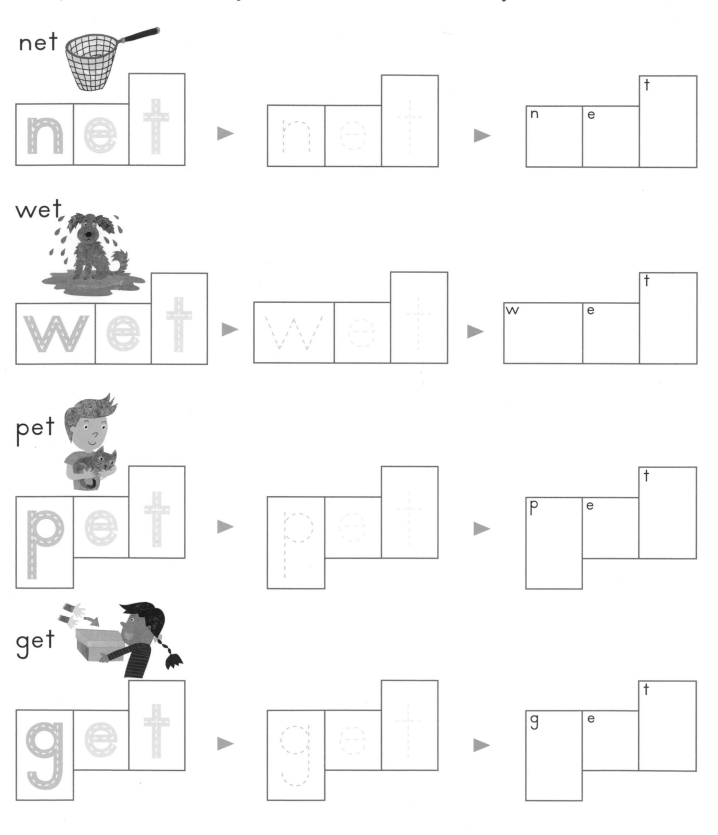

net

wet

pet

get

16 Review

Saying "_en" and "_et" Words

Name

Date

- Draw a line from 👦 to 👦 while saying each "_en" word.

  Draw a line from 👧 to 👧 while saying each "_et" word.

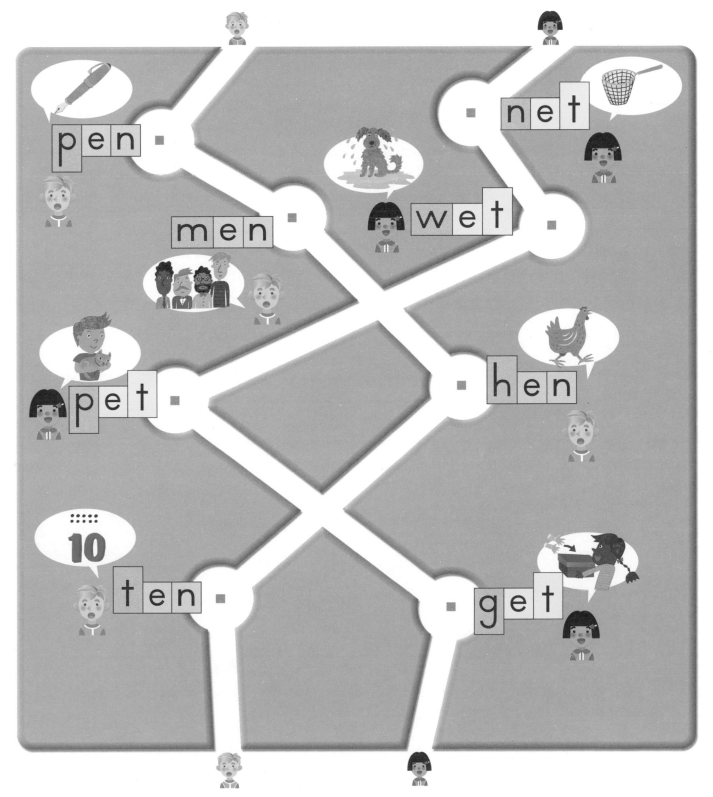

Writing "_en" and "_et" Words

■ Say the word. Then say the sound of each letter as you write it.

pen

| p | e | n |

net

| n | e | t |

men

| m | e | n |

wet

| w | e | t |

hen

| h | | |
| | e | n |

pet

| p | e | t |

ten

| t | | |
| | e | n |

get

| g | e | t |

What Is It?

Saying "_ig" Sounds

To parents
By repeating rhyming words, your child will gain an awareness of the connection between letters and the sounds they represent.

Name

Date

■ Match the pictures by drawing a line from the dot (●) to the star (★).

 ●

★  pig

 ●

★  wig

 ●

★  dig

 ●

★  big

■ Draw a line from the dot (●) to the star (★) while saying each word.

Rhyming Words
Writing "_ig" Words

Name

Date

■ Say the word. Then say the sound of each letter as you trace it.

pig

pig ▶ pig ▶ pig

wig

wig ▶ wig ▶ wig

dig

dig ▶ dig ▶ dig

big

big ▶ big ▶ big

■ Say the word. Then say the sound of each letter as you trace and write it.

pig

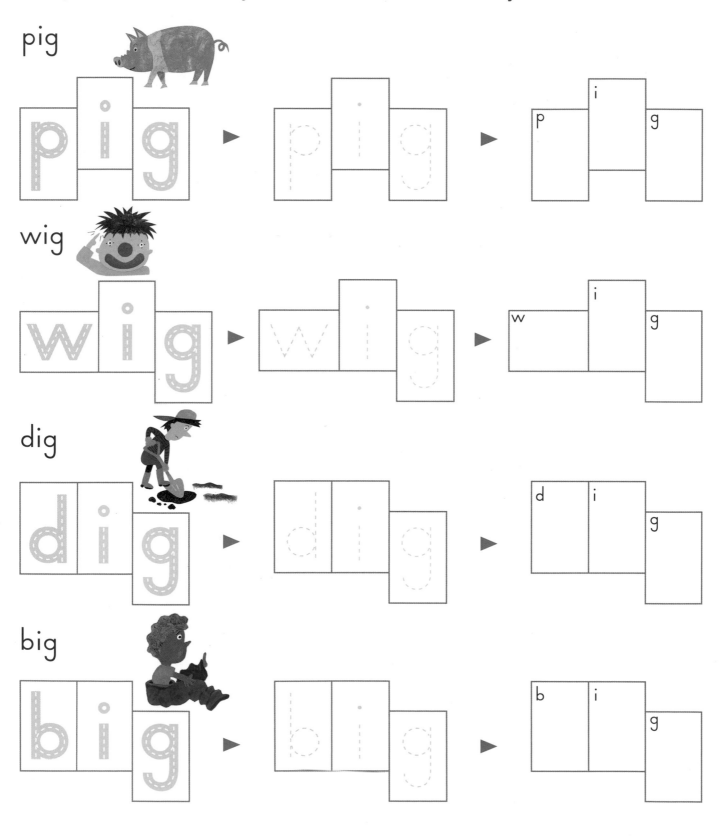

wig

dig

big

What Is It?
Saying "_in" Sounds

Name

Date

■ Match the pictures by drawing a line from the dot (●) to the star (★).

 ●

★  bin

 ●

★ tin

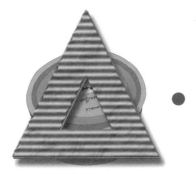 ●

★ pin

 ●

★ fin

■ Draw a line from the dot (●) to the star (★) while saying each word.

Rhyming Words
Writing "_in" Words

Name

Date

■ Say the word. Then say the sound of each letter as you trace it.

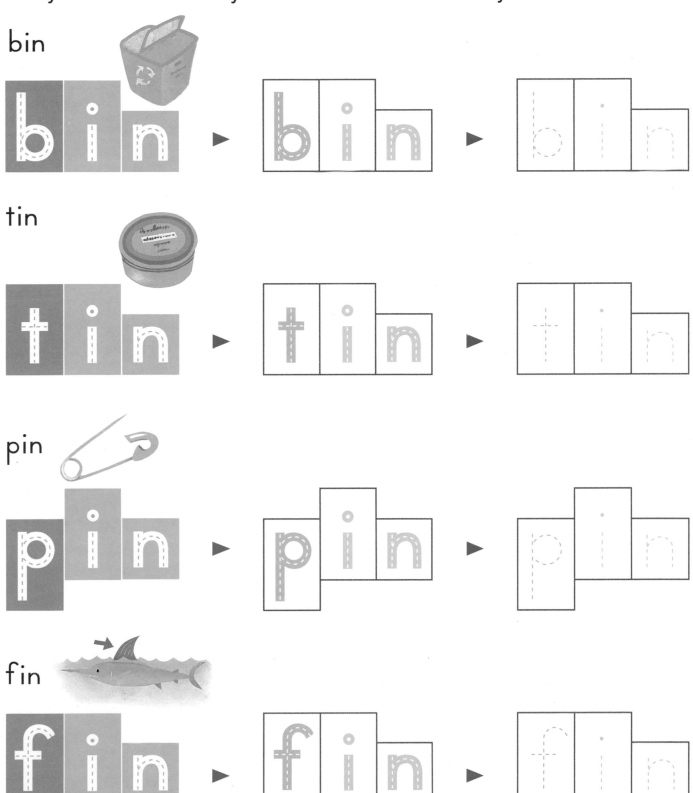

bin

tin

pin

fin

■ Say the word. Then say the sound of each letter as you trace and write it.

bin

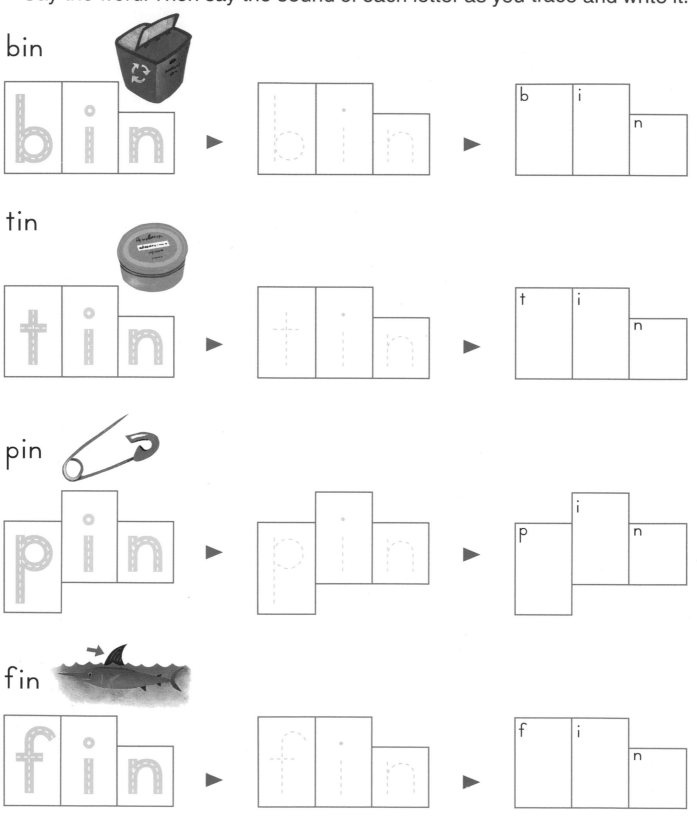

tin

pin

fin

What Is It?

Saying "_ip" Sounds

■ Match the pictures by drawing a line from the dot (●) to the star (★).

 ●

★  hip

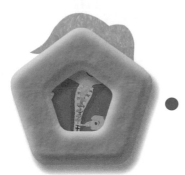 ●

★  lip

 ●

★  zip

 ●

★  rip

■ Draw a line from the dot (●) to the star (★) while saying each word.

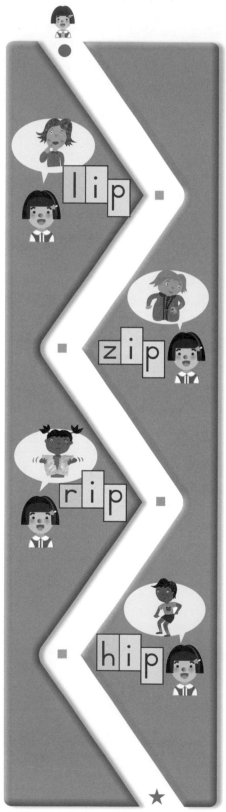

Rhyming Words
Writing "_ip" Words

Name

Date

■ Say the word. Then say the sound of each letter as you trace it.

hip

h i p ▶ **h i p** ▶ h i p

lip

l i p ▶ **l i p** ▶ l i p

zip

z i p ▶ **z i p** ▶ z i p

rip

r i p ▶ **r i p** ▶ r i p

Writing "_ip" Words

■ Say the word. Then say the sound of each letter as you trace and write it.

hip

lip

zip

rip

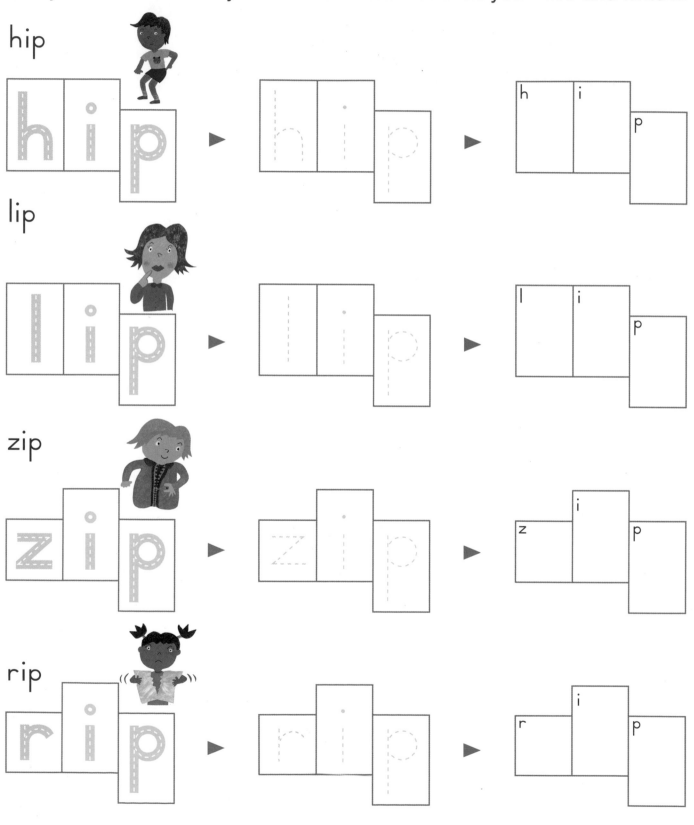

Review

Saying "_ig" and "_in" Words

■ Draw a line from 👦 to 👦 while saying each "_ig" word.

Draw a line from 👧 to 👧 while saying each "_in" word.

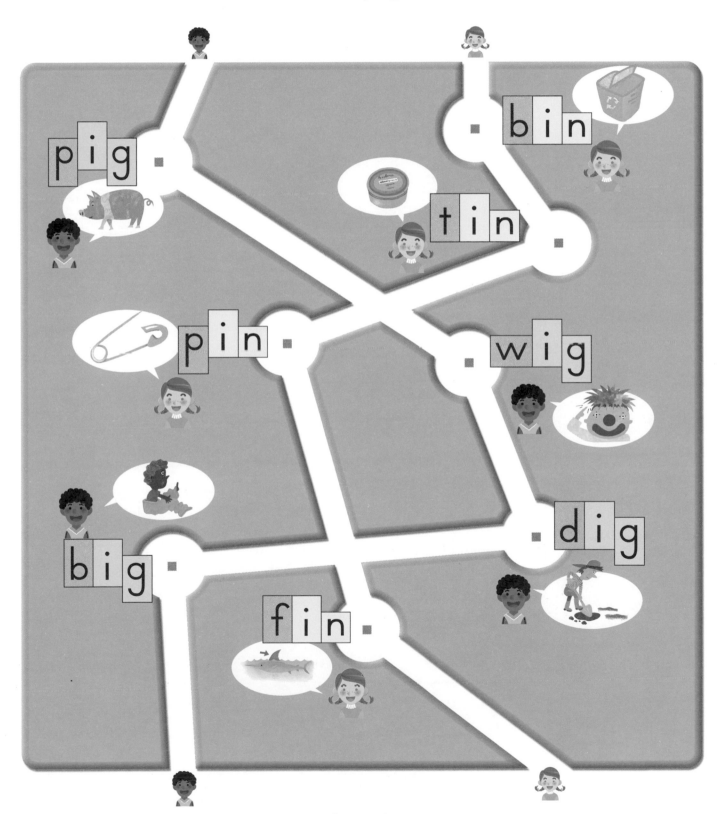

Writing "_ig" and "_in" Words

■ Say the word. Then say the sound of each letter as you write it.

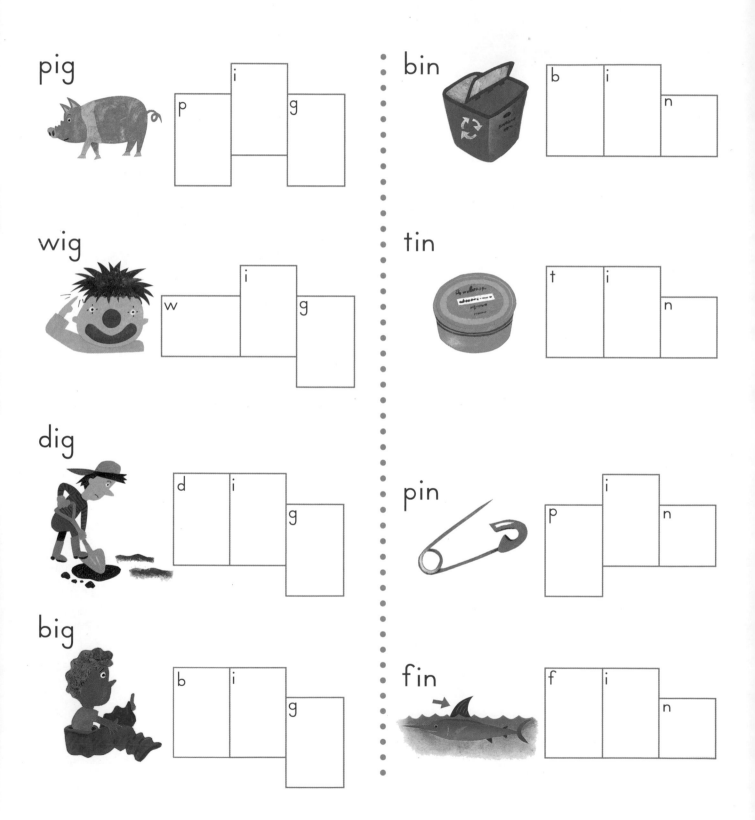

pig

	i	
p		g

bin

b	i	
		n

wig

	i	
w		g

tin

t	i	
		n

dig

d	i	
		g

pin

	i	
p		n

big

b	i	
		g

fin

f	i	
		n

24 Review
Saying "_ip" and "_ig" Words

Name

Date

■ Draw a line from 🧒 to 🧒 while saying each "_ip" word.
　Draw a line from 🧒 to 🧒 while saying each "_ig" word.

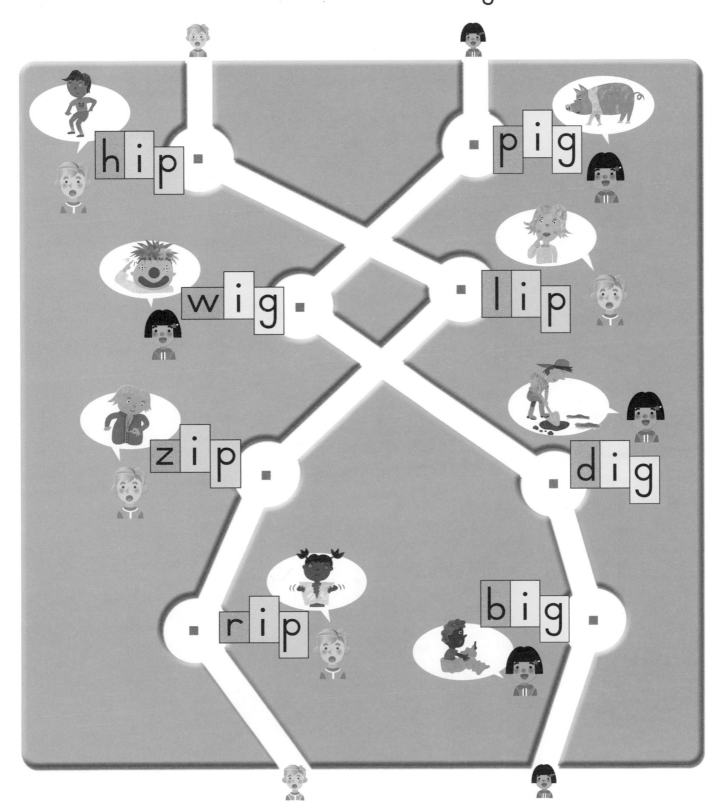

Writing "_ip" and "_ig" Words

■ Say the word. Then say the sound of each letter as you write it.

hip

| h | i |
| p |

pig

| | i |
| p | g |

lip

| l | i |
| p |

wig

| | i |
| w | g |

zip

| | i |
| z | p |

dig

| d | i |
| g |

rip

| | i |
| r | p |

big

| b | i |
| g |

What Is It?

Saying "_op" Sounds

Name

Date

■ Match the pictures by drawing a line from the dot (●) to the star (★).

 ●

★ 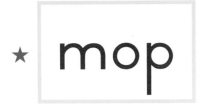  mop

 ●

★  top

 ●

★  hop

 ●

★  pop

■ Draw a line from the dot (●) to the star (★) while saying each word.

26 Rhyming Words
Writing "_op" Words

Name

Date

■ Say the word. Then say the sound of each letter as you trace it.

mop

top

hop

pop

■ Say the word. Then say the sound of each letter as you trace and write it.

mop

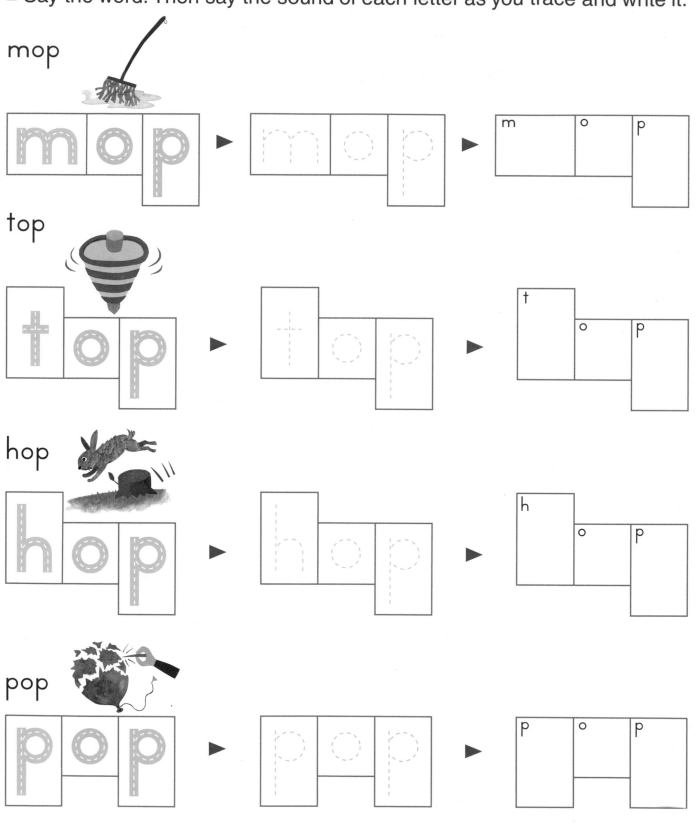

top

hop

pop

What Is It?
Saying "_og" Sounds

Name

Date

■ Match the pictures by drawing a line from the dot (●) to the star (★).

●  ★ **dog**

●  ★ **log**

●  ★ **hog**

●  ★ **jog**

■ Draw a line from the dot (●) to the star (★) while saying each word.

28 Rhyming Words
Writing "_og" Words

Name

Date

■ Say the word. Then say the sound of each letter as you trace it.

dog ▶

log ▶

hog ▶

jog ▶

■ Say the word. Then say the sound of each letter as you trace and write it.

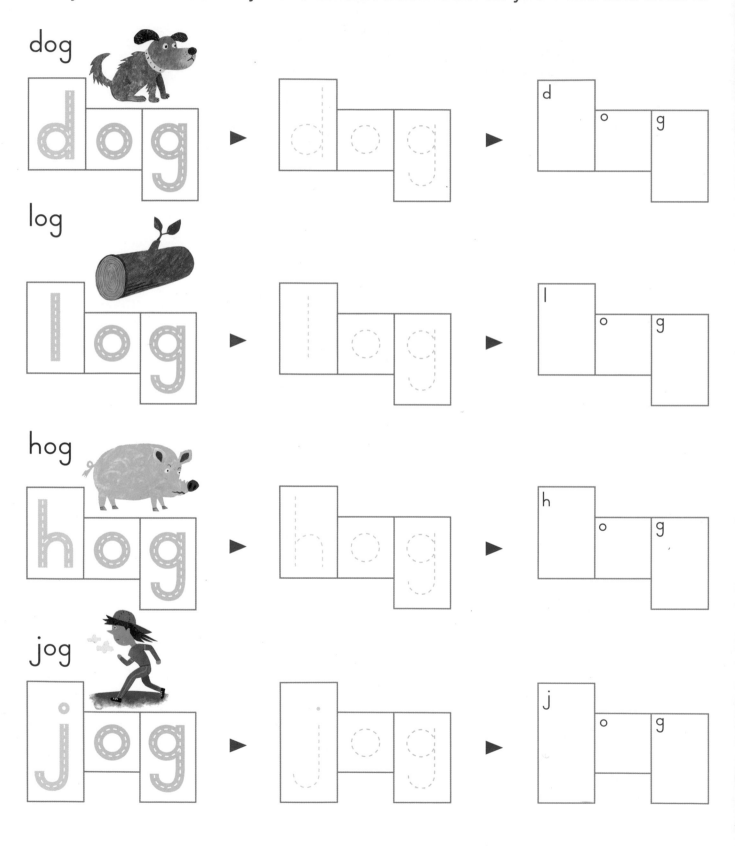

dog

log

hog

jog

 **Review**

Saying "_op" and "_og" Words

Name
Date

■ Draw a line from 👦 to 👦 while saying each "_op" word.
Draw a line from 👧 to 👧 while saying each "_og" word.

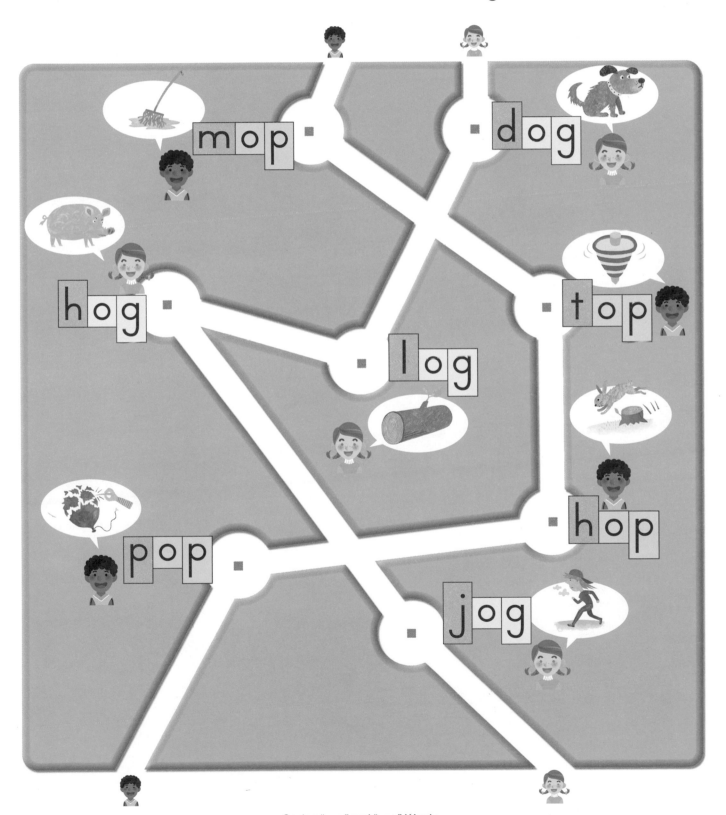

Writing "_op" and "_og" Words

■ Say the word. Then say the sound of each letter as you write it.

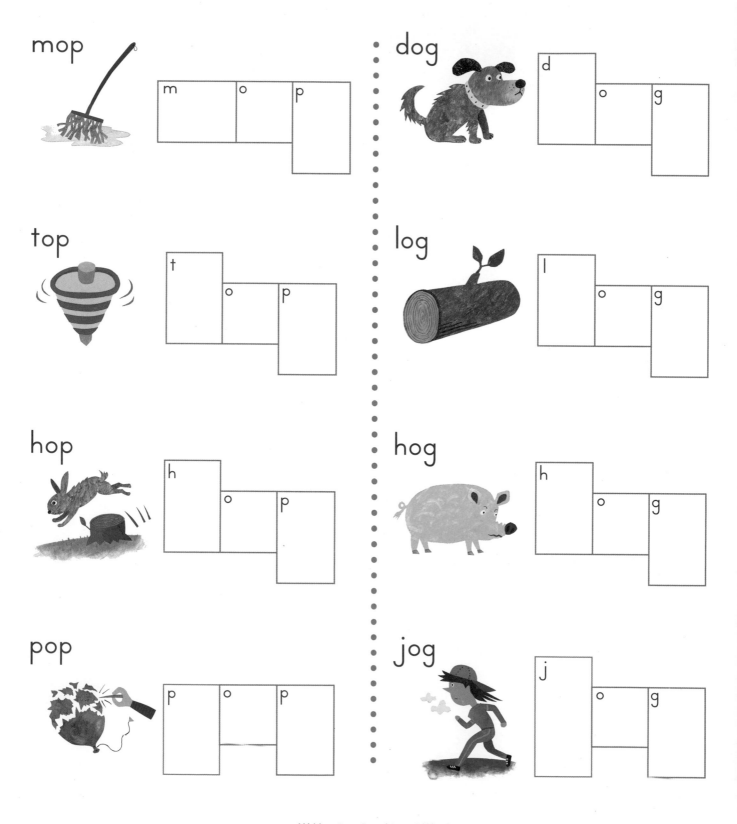

mop

| m | o | p |

top

| t | o | p |

hop

| h | o | p |

pop

| p | o | p |

dog

| d | o | g |

log

| l | o | g |

hog

| h | o | g |

jog

| j | o | g |

30 What Is It?
Saying "_ug" Sounds

Name

Date

■ Match the pictures by drawing a line from the dot (●) to the star (★).

   ●

★  bug

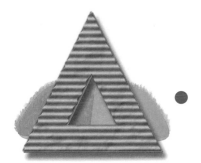   ●

★  mug

   ●

★  hug

   ●

★  rug

■ Draw a line from the dot (●) to the star (★) while saying each word.

31 Rhyming Words
Writing "_ug" Words

Name

Date

■ Say the word. Then say the sound of each letter as you trace it.

bug

bug ▶ **bug** ▶ bug

mug

mug ▶ **mug** ▶ mug

hug

hug ▶ **hug** ▶ hug

rug

rug ▶ **rug** ▶ rug

■ Say the word. Then say the sound of each letter as you trace and write it.

bug

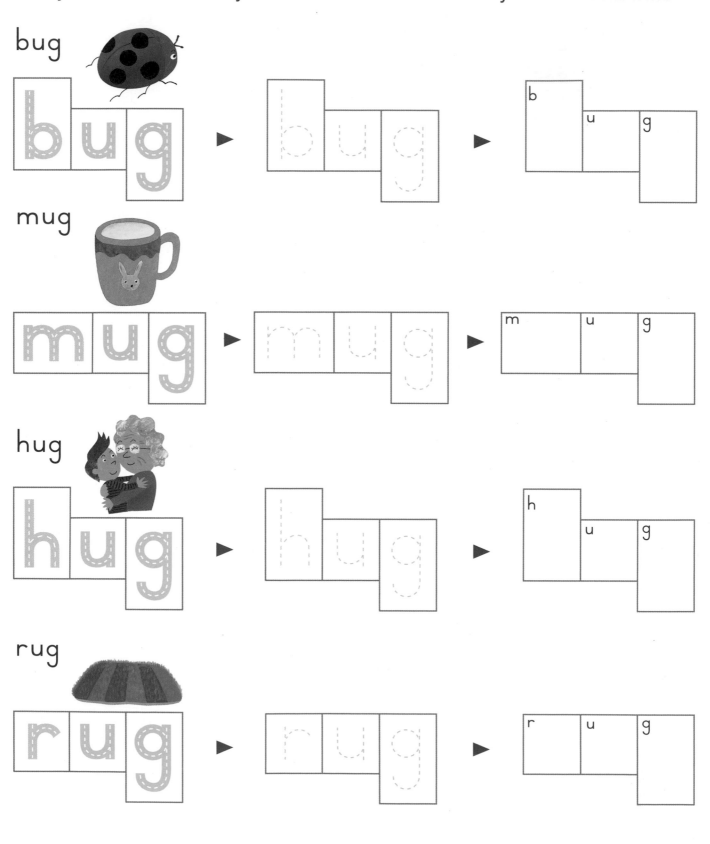

mug

hug

rug

32 What Is It?

Saying "_un" Sounds

Name

Date

■ Match the pictures by drawing a line from the dot (●) to the star (★).

 ●

★  sun

 ●

★  bun

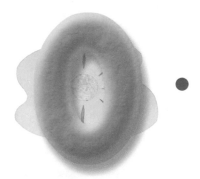 ●

★  run

 ●

★  fun

■ Draw a line from the dot (●) to the star (★) while saying each word.

33 Rhyming Words
Writing "_un" Words

Name

Date

■ Say the word. Then say the sound of each letter as you trace it.

sun

 ▶ 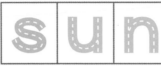 ▶

bun

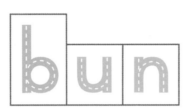 ▶ ▶

run

 ▶ ▶

fun

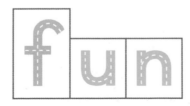 ▶  ▶

■ Say the word. Then say the sound of each letter as you trace and write it.

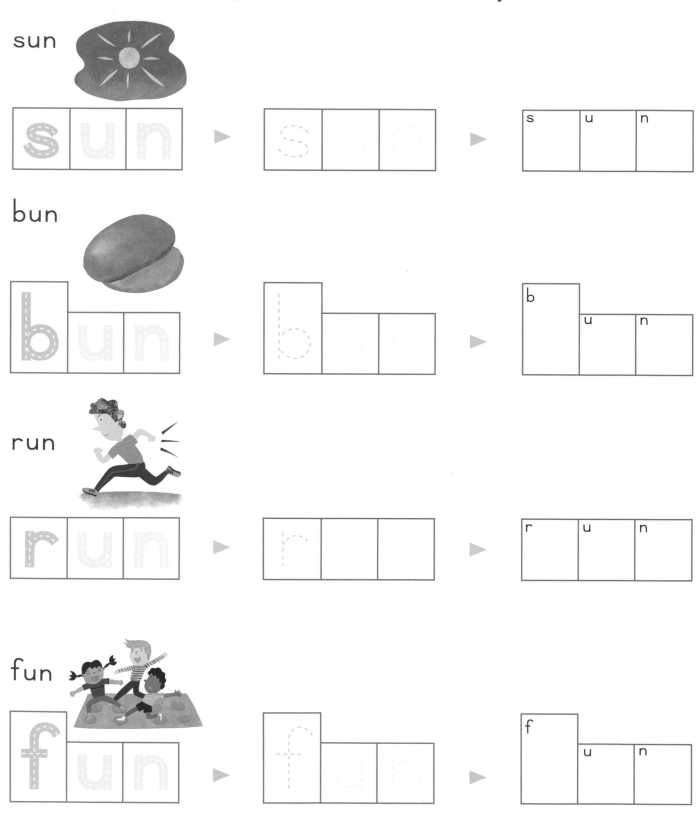

sun

bun

run

fun

Review

Saying "_ug" and "_un" Words

Name

Date

■ Draw a line from 🧑 to 🧑 while saying each "_ug" word.

Draw a line from 👧 to 👧 while saying each "_un" word.

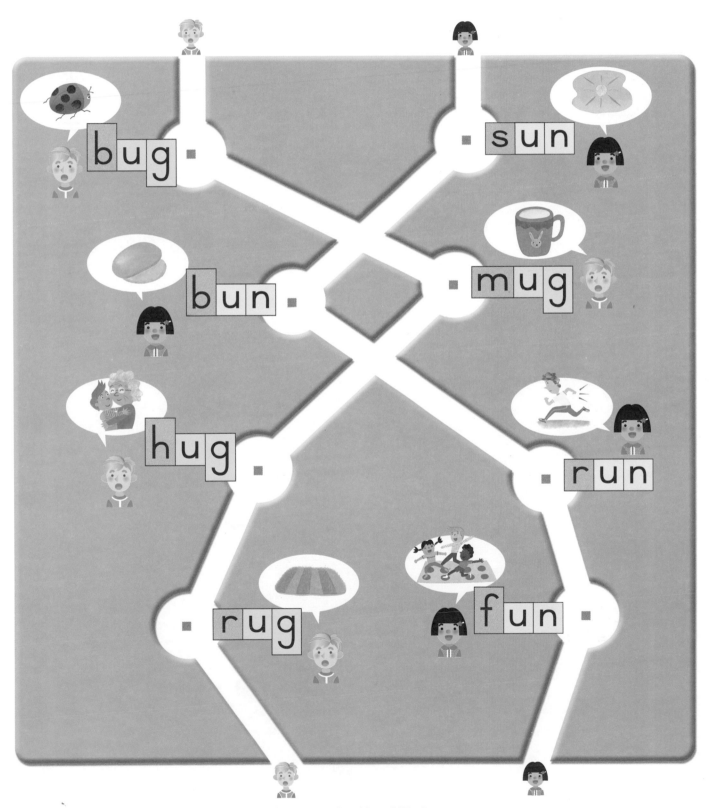

Writing "_ug" and "_un" Words

■ Say the word. Then say the sound of each letter as you write it.

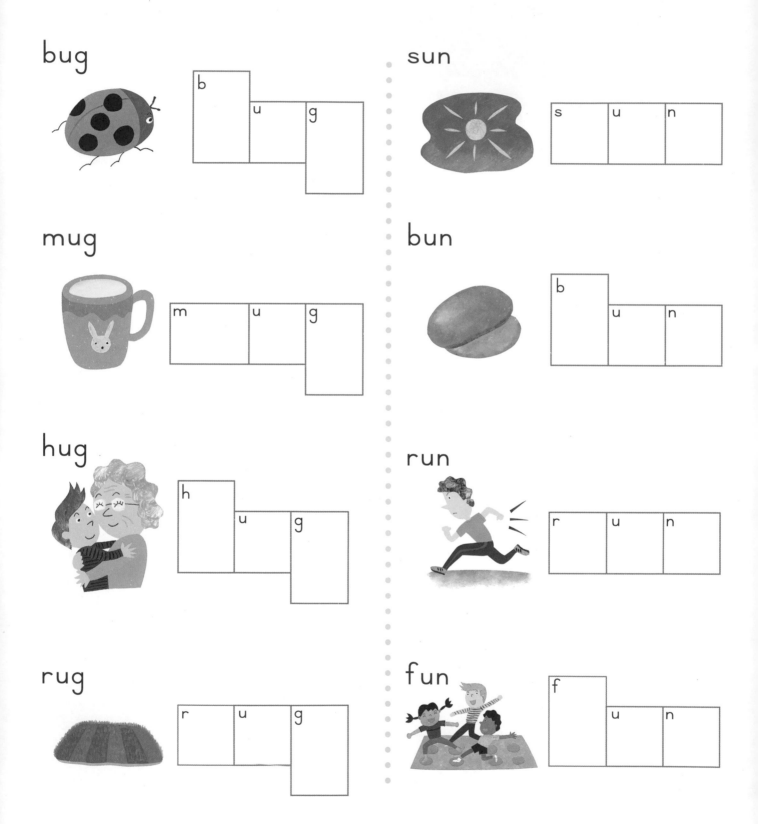

bug

b		
	u	g

sun

| s | u | n |

mug

| m | u | g |

bun

b		
	u	n

hug

h		
	u	g

run

| r | u | n |

rug

| r | u | g |

fun

f		
	u	n

Review
Saying "_at" Words

Name

Date

To parents
Your child should connect the "rat" to the "cat" again to begin another sequence. Make sure your child draws vertical or horizontal lines, not diagonal ones.

■ Draw a line from the arrow (→) to the star (★),

connecting  to bat to hat to rat while you say the words.

cat   bat   hat   rat

man	can	pan	fan	cat
bat	cat	rat	hat	bat
hat	fan	man	pan	can
rat	cat	bat	hat	rat
fan	pan	fan	man	cat
man	can	cat	pan	bat

Writing "_at" and "_an" Words

■ Say the word. Then say the sound of each letter as you write it.

cat

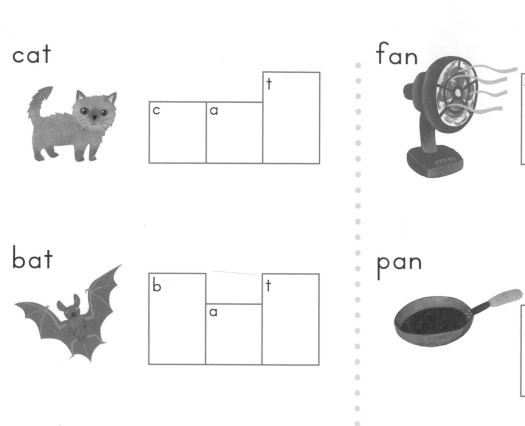

c	a	t

fan

f	a	n

bat

b	a	t

pan

p	a	n

hat

h	a	t

can

c	a	n

man

m	a	n

rat

r	a	t

36 Review
Saying "_ap" Words

Name

Date

To parents
Your child should connect the "tap" to the "cap" again to begin another sequence. Make sure your child draws vertical or horizontal lines, not diagonal ones.

■ Draw a line from the arrow (→) to the star (★), connecting [cap] to [map] to [nap] to [tap] while you say the words.

Writing "_ap" and "_ad" Words

■ Say the word. Then say the sound of each letter as you write it.

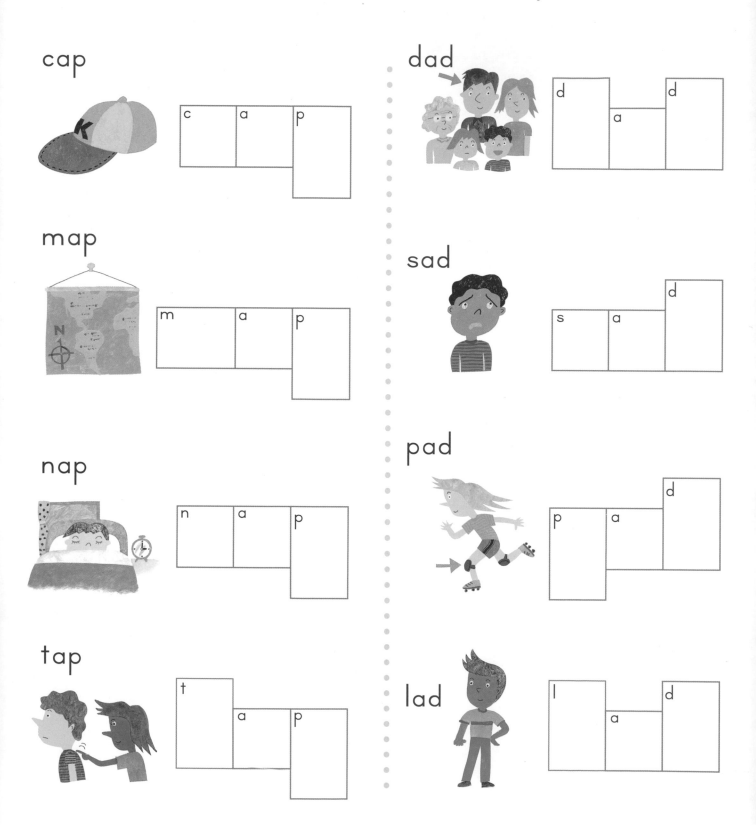

cap

| c | a | p |

map

| m | a | p |

nap

| n | a | p |

tap

| t | | |
| | a | p |

dad

| d | | d |
| | a | |

sad

| | | d |
| s | a | |

pad

| | | d |
| p | a | |

lad

| l | | d |
| | a | |

Review
Saying "_en" Words

Name

Date

To parents
Your child should connect the "ten" to the "pen" again to begin another sequence. Make sure your child draws vertical or horizontal lines, not diagonal ones.

■ Draw a line from the arrow (→) to the star (★),

connecting 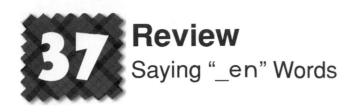 while you say the words.

pen   men   hen   ten

pen	ten 10	hen	men	pen
men	wet	get	pet	net
hen	ten 10	pen	men	wet
net	get	net	hen	pet
hen	pet	get	ten 10	pen
pet	wet	men	net	men

Writing "_en" and "_et" Words

■ Say the word. Then say the sound of each letter as you write it.

pen

p	e	n

net

n	e	t

men

m	e	n

wet

w	e	t

hen

h		
	e	n

pet

p	e	t

ten

t		
	e	n

get

g	e	t

Review
Saying "_in" Words

Name

Date

To parents
Your child should connect the "fin" to the "bin" again to
begin another sequence. Make sure your child draws
vertical or horizontal lines, not diagonal ones.

■ Draw a line from the arrow (→) to the star (★),

connecting [bin] to [tin] to [pin] to [fin] while you say the words.

bin　　tin　　pin　　fin

zip	lip	hip	tin	bin
rip	bin	fin	pin	rip
zip	tin	zip	hip	lip
hip	pin	fin	bin	tin
bin	lip	rip	hip	pin
rip	pin	zip	lip	fin

Writing "_in" and "_ip" Words

■ Say the word. Then say the sound of each letter as you write it.

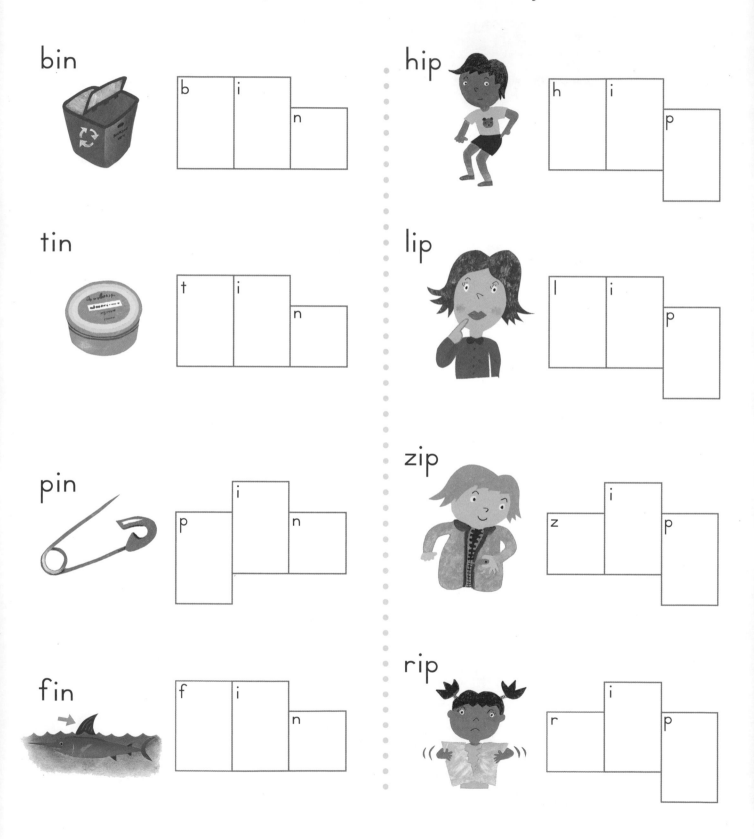

bin

b	i	
		n

hip

h	i	
		p

tin

t	i	
		n

lip

l	i	
		p

pin

	i	
p		n

zip

	i	
z		p

fin

f	i	
		n

rip

	i	
r		p

Review

Saying "_op" Words

Name

Date

To parents
Your child should connect the "pop" to the "mop" again to begin another sequence. Make sure your child draws vertical or horizontal lines, not diagonal ones.

■ Draw a line from the arrow (→) to the star (★),

connecting 🧹 to 🪀 to 🐰 to 🎈 while you say the words.

mop   top   hop   pop

↓

mop	pop	hop	top	mop
top	dog	log	hog	jog
hop	pop	mop	top	hop
log	hog	dog	jog	pop
mop	pop	jog	log	mop
top	log	dog	hog	top

★

Writing "_op" and "_og" Words

■ Say the word. Then say the sound of each letter as you write it.

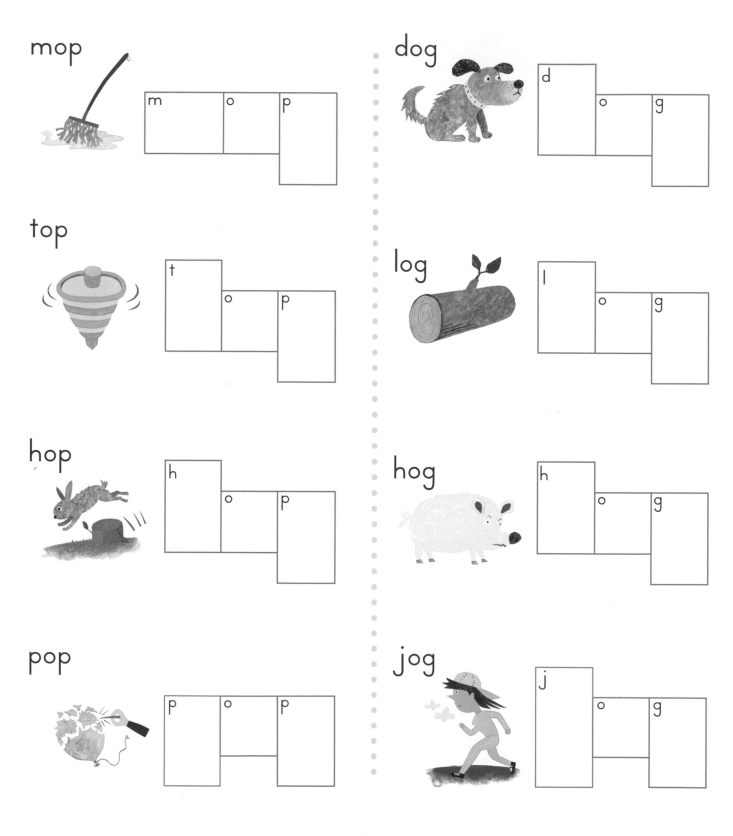

mop

| m | o | p |

dog

| d | o | g |

top

| t | o | p |

log

| l | o | g |

hop

| h | o | p |

hog

| h | o | g |

pop

| p | o | p |

jog

| j | o | g |

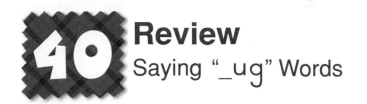

Review

Saying "_ug" Words

<table>
<tr><td>Name</td></tr>
<tr><td>Date</td></tr>
</table>

To parents
Your child should connect the "rug" to the "bug" again to begin another sequence. Make sure your child draws vertical or horizontal lines, not diagonal ones.

■ Draw a line from the arrow (→) to the star (★), connecting 🐞 to ☕ to 👵 to 〰️ while you say the words.

bug   mug   hug   rug

↓

bun	sun	run	fun	bug
mug	bug	rug	hug	mug
hug	fun	sun	bun	fun
rug	bug	mug	hug	rug
bun	sun	fun	run	bug
fun	bug	run	sun	mug

★

Writing "_ug" and "_un" Words

To parents
Your child has been developing phonemic awareness skills, which are necessary building blocks to learning how to sound out words and to read. Please encourage your child and nurture a lifelong love of reading.

■ Say the word. Then say the sound of each letter as you write it.

bug

mug

hug

rug

sun

bun

run

fun

You are now able to say and write short rhyming words.
Congratulations!

Certificate of Achievement

is hereby congratulated on completing

My Book of Rhyming Words

Presented on _____ , 20 ____

_____
Parent or Guardian

cat bat hat